THE VALAC CREATION

SPOOKYPUPPET

ISBN 979-888569116-1

Contents

THE VOLAC CREATION

ONE

1920 Romania

Maria born to a convent family, was a true devoti of God, and wanted to be the messenger of God. Being a toddler, she followed all the rules and regulation of being a Nun and also, followed the teachings of Bible. Maria enjoyed going to school as she was the most brightest and obedient ones among all.

As she grew up, she started ministering the word of God in a very young age. Her parents and society admired her faith in God, and her being such devoted to God. Maria's life was completely different from other girls of her age, as she believed that her life was only meant to do the work of God.

1940 Twenty years later.
Maria was an adult now, and was recognised as sister maria. Her faith in God turned her life into a very important person for the society, she was treated like a member of royal family, as her act of kindness was very pleasing to the society, her prayers were strong enough to heal a sick man. The priest of the church counted her as one of the head member of the church, for she was one of the nobel Nun. Maria was still incomplete on her journey

to become the messenger of God, as she had much more to know about God.

1945 Five years later .

Maria was now educated enough to be the messenger of God, as her journey was partly accomplished. One day, maria was teaching about the Bible to the young ones at the church, a man with a long white outfit stand outside the door was watching maria teaching the young ones. Maria observed the man looking at her, the man called her by waving his hand to her with a smile on his face. Maria went to check who the man was, and then she asked him "who are you Father, are you looking for someone?" The man replied "yes. I was looking for you maria, my father sent me here, I came from a very far place just too see you." "But, how do you know me father?"

Asked Maria. "I've known you already, Your faith in God gave me your way, and i'm here to tell you that you've been chosen maria, and your journey starts from today." Replied the man. "I'm confused, I don't understand what your saying and I don't know who are you?" Replied maria. "Wait untill the right time comes maria, you will certainly understand everything. I will appear to you untill your journey is full accomplished." The man said that and walked away.

As Maria was walking back, sister Rita stoped her on the way and asked "whom were you talking to Maria?" In a very confusing way maria replies "I was talking to that father, he said he came from a very place just to see me. It was hard to understand what he said to me. "Sister Rita was shocked listening to her statement, and asks her "are you alright

Maria? Is everything fine with you.?" " yes I'm fine."

One week later Maria was lying on her bed and trying to fall asleep, moments later a bright light appeared in her room, she could feel the beam with her eyes closed, as she opend her eyes to see what it was, the light took a form of a figure, she saw that it was the same father whom she met a week before.

Maria had no clue on things happening to her, she had nothing to talk. "You have a long journey to go Maria, your life is now going to change, you shall do miracles to people as your wish has been granted." Said the man,
And disappeared.

Maria wanted to inform the high priest about things happening to her, as she felt something is haunting her. Next day maria went to the church to meet father Erric, she told everything to him, about the man who appeared to her. "Are you alright maria?" asked father Erric. "I'm fine" said maria. "Sister Rita told me that you we're speaking to yourself yesterday." "No I was speaking to that father" "who is that father you were speaking too maria?" "I don't know, I didn't ask his name. He suddenly appears and then disappears."

"Maria i'm now worried about you, i'm afraid if anything is trying to latch onto you, come with me maria." Said father Erric. Father Erric gave her a holy water, and asked her to sprinkle it in her room. He also, told her that he would pray for her. Next day sister Rita visits maria, "did you visit father Erric yesterday?" Asked sister Rita. "Yes I did, and he said that you told him that I was speaking to my self outside the church." Replied maria. "Yes I told father Erric that, intact that's why I asked you, whom were you talking to. Is everything alright maria.?" Maria with quavering voice said "I really don't know what's happening."

One day while attending service at church, maria saw the same man walking around outside the church. Maria furiously rushed out to chek on him, but by the she reached out he wasn't there. Maria was looking for him in and around the church, and found him in the backyard of the church standing beneath a tree. "Father" called out maria. "What are you doing here?" Asked maria. "I told you maria that I will appear to you constantly, until your journey is fully accomplished." Said the man. Maria confusingly asked "but who are you father ?, I certainly don't understand what is happening." In a euphonious voice the man replied "my parents named me emmanuel, but people calls unto me by the name Jesus." As the man said that a shining light emanated from his body, she couldn't stand the light and fainted.

Later sister Rita was looking for maria, and found her lying unconscious in the backyard of the church. Sister Rita panicked, and immediately ran to her and started to wake her up. "Maria...maria... What happened to you, how did you faint?" Maria woke up from unconsciousness and told sister Rita "the man who often appears to me is non another then Jesus himself, I saw it, a bright light emanated from his body and I fainted." "What are you talking maria, are you on your senses?" Asked sister Rita "I'm totally fine, and I'm serious about it."

Next day sister Rita visited father Erric, and told him

everything about maria. "I'm afraid she could fall in some kind of trouble, for her being such a devoted soul." Said father Erric.
"But I still couldn't believe that, when she told me that the man was jesus.?" Asked sister Rita. " we
may not know what she is exactly undergoing, this could be an act from both the sides either the good
or the bad side. But I'm sure something is trying to test faith or perhaps attack. "

December fifteen, preparations was going on in the church for christmas, and next day was healing
sunday, as many disabled people would come with there healing prayers. The society, believed that
miracles are more powerful then treatments.

The day of healing sunday, many disabled people came to the church from different towns, everyone
gathered as one and the priest started to do the healing prayers. Maria was also, doing her prayer with
her eyes closed, and suddenly she heard a voice of a man calling her, " maria...maria...." Maria
immediately opend her eyes and looked around to see for the unknown voice, and found nothing
suspicious. Moments later she heard the voice again, and this time a figure magically appeared, and
she saw it was Jesus. He said to her " the time has come maria, i told you, you're gifted and you shall
now do miracles, go heal them with your faith for the lord is with you."

A lady brought her fifteen year old paralyzed son on a wheelchair to maria, and the lady started crying

on her knees begging maria to pray for her son. Maria almost cried looking at that poor little boy, and
the she heard his voice again, " your faith can change anything maria, believe it and you will see it."
Maria took the holy water and raised it above and started to pray for the boy, she sprinkled the holy
water on both his legs and said " in the name of the father , son and the holy spirit you shall now stand
on your feet.

Maria asked everyone to move a side and asked the boy to stand on his feet , there was complete
silence in the room and the boy slowly stood up and walked towards his mother. The mother couldn't
believe, his son who sat for fifteen years was finally able to stand on his feet. She couldn't stop
sobbing and thanked maria. And so on maria heald all the disabled people. Maria's life totally changed
after that day, she was very well protected and given a separate royal stay next to the abbey.

Five days left for christmas, everyone was busy with some or the other church chores. Maria was
reading her Bible in her room, and while reading she heard someone calling her, and she turned to see,
it was Jesus. In a dulcet voice maria said "father, I thought you disappeared and would never appear
again." "I told you I will appear until your journey is accomplished maria." "But I feel, my journey is
accomplished Now." Said maria " there is more to it maria, there is one last deed that needs to be
done, and then your journey will be accomplished." "What is it father?"

He gave her a spell written on a piece of paper and said "maria this spell is very powerful, which will
keep all the evil away from you, and you have to cast the spell."

"But why should I cast it father." Asked maria "maria in this journey there will be many evil that will try
block your way's, with the help of this spell you will call a holy spirit that will protect you from evil."
"But when and how do I cast it father?" Asked maria "don't open the spell now, cast it on the day before
christmas, wait until the night fall, burn appropriate candles and incense, join your hands and cast the
spell. Once the ritual is completed the holy spirit will appear to you. And on the day of christmas,
everyone will be able to see me in your form." He said that and disappeared. At some point maria was
also confused about the spell, but anyhow she decided to cast the spell.

The night of twenty-fourth, she did the set-up for the ritual as she was asked to. The clock struck to
twelve sharp she sat down and started to slowly chant the spell, and then she realised the spell that
she is chanting, is not to call the holy spirit perhaps she was inviting a cruel demon and sacrificing her
life. But unfortunately she couldn't stop chanting the spell, she felt someone has a control over her.
Things around started to levitate, she was feeling apprehensive but was unable to do anything.

She saw a figure magically appearing in front of her, she saw a dark figure walking towards her, and when it came a bit closer she saw it was Jesus. The figure levitated and appeared in his real form. It appeared to be a young demon boy with angle wings ridding on a two headed dragon. Seeing that bloodcurdling scene, maria's heartbeat raised and her chanting became faster She was now helpless. As the figure kept forming bigger, everything around started to hurl automatically. And then the demon immediately took maria under his control.

then the demon entered maria's body through her mouth and completely subdued her.

Next day sister Rita went to maria's room to call her, she knocked at the door but maria didn't open the door, sister Rita was then forced to enter her room, she couldn't believe what she saw. She saw that maria's body was completely deformed lying on bed, out of fear Rita screamed loudly hearing her scream rest of the nun rushed from the abbey to see what happened. Immediately than father Erric was called, when he saw gee he had no reaction on his face, but said "that happened what is was afraid of." "What happened father?" Asked Sister Rita, "she is possessed, the man who appeared to her was a demon who successfully fooled her, and possessed her. Everyone was shocked when they heard that Sister maria was possessed."Bring her to the church" said father Erric. Almost entire town gathered in and around the church, when they heard the messenger of god was possessed.

Possessed maria's deformed body was brought to the

church, and was kept in front of the statue of
christ. Father Erric told that he would perform exorcism to
cast out the demon from maria's body, but
he was not aware that, what kind of evil power he had to
battle with. While everyone watched him, he
took his Bible and the holy water and started to read the
versus from Bible loudly. As he kept reading,
moments later maria's deformed body was now forming
normal and she started to levitate. Everyone
around panicked, slowly maria's eyes opened and there was
a scarry smile on her face. Father Erric
knew it was the devil, he begins to read the Bible loudly and
sprinkles holy water on her. With a scarry
smile the devil said "your abilities and power's are futile in
front of me, she is mine." Father Erric
fiercely asked "what is your name demon?" "I'm the high
president of hell and the ruler of the demon
horde, I am volac."

The demon flung father Erric against the wall and escaped,
in harrowing voice father Erric said "its too
late now the demon is very powerful." Immediately father
Erric was hospitalized "nothing will happen
to you father, you will be alright." Said sister Rita.

" I know I'm not going to live, I knew something was trying
to test her faith, but I wasn't sure. Forgive
me my sins lord." Unfortunately father Erric died. Sister
Rita hears a loud screaming voice of another
sister from the backyard, she immediately rushes to see
what happened. She saw maria's dead body
was lying beneath the tree, maria couldn't stop sobbing.

Later the church member's buried both father Erric and sister Maria. There was statue of maria built
upon her gave, and the grave stone read "the possessed Nun sis.Maria 1920-1945." After one year of
sister Maria's death, the Nun's said that they often see sister Maria's apparition at the abbey which
haunted other Nun's.